UNIFORMS PROVIDED

UNIFORMS PROVIDED

JAMES A MOORE

To order additional copies of this book, contact:
Xlibris
1-888-795-4274
www.Xlibris.com
Orders@Xlibris.com
746428

Contents

Chapter 1

The Call

"And how old might ya be?" the sergeant behind the desk responded.

"I'm over eighteen," responded George, holding his hat in his hand and looking down toward his brogans, a heavy ankle-high work shoe. George was almost six feet tall. With his deep-set hazel eyes and his serious facial expression, he always looked older than his sixteen years. His self-respect turned upside down after his encounter with the army's physicians. The doctor had them strip down and then jump up and down. Then he looked for any tumors. Finally, he wanted to see if each recruit had free use of all his limbs. Directly in front of him, George heard the doctor declare to his orderly, "This man is a 4-F. Disqualified."

"What's that mean?" George asked another recruit beside him.

"Well, if you ain't got your four front teeth, you can't tear open the cartridge with the gunpowder and the bullet. Land sakes! What good are you if you can't load and shoot?"

George's clothing was as mixed as his emotions from his store-bought pants to the ruffled shirt his sister had made for him.

"Well, you're in," the sergeant said. "Now wait outside with the others."

In the waiting area, a freckled red-haired boy whistled through the gap in his front teeth as he approached George. "Did it work?" he asked.

"I suppose," George said as he took off a brogan and pulled the paper out with the number eighteen written on it.

"Name's William Baker. What's yours?"

"George Everson."

"Ya see," William continued, "you weren't really telling a lie. You were *over* eighteen. Leastwise, you were standing over it when you put that there piece of paper in your shoe with the number eighteen on it."

"Well, I guess. If they find out, then what will they do?" George pondered, passing his fingers through his full, curly black hair, his hat still in his other hand.

"Kick us out, I reckon. Nevertheless, no one will unless we tell someone we're only sixteen. I sure do want to get into the mess of this fray," William declared.

George agreed. He wanted to get into the war too. He couldn't remember when he had not been behind a plow. When he had seen the announcement in the local newspaper the fever began.

MORE VOLUNTEERS ACCEPTED.

GENERAL BURNSIDE'S COAST DIVISION to which

GENERAL RENO'S brigade is attached. The Fifty-

first NEW YORK VOLUNTEERS commanded by that

excellent officer, COLONEL WILLIAM FERRERO.

A grand opportunity is afforded for patriotic persons

to enlist in the service of their country under the

command of as able officers as the country has yet

furnished.

UNIFORMS ALSO PROVIDED.

George had continued reading, thinking about Sarah and Jane, his sisters, and his brother, John. He thought about his last conversation with his father, who was the volunteer preacher for the area. Money was hard to come by for the family, and times were tough. Offerings and collections were never enough to support a full-time preacher.

"You're not old enough, son," his father's words still echoed in his mind. George felt he had to do something, but he simply could not see himself behind a plow for the rest of his life. He wanted something different. He wanted to contribute to his family another way. There had to be an opportunity to lift himself out of the farm. At the same time, he wanted to experience new adventures. Something was out there besides boring farm life.

It was now up to George Everson to make a difference. The fever was at a high pitch when he read the note attached at the bottom.

$578.00 for twenty-one months of service.

$252.00 state aid for families of four.

$830.50 and short service and

$125.00 cash in hand.

—September 12, 1861

How that money would help, he pondered. The excitement stirred in his head. He would never see this much money so fast on the farm. *Maybe,* he thought, *with over a thousand dollars, I could get into a nice school and get to study all those great books and authors I've been hearing about. Maybe become a lawyer, doctor, anything but farming. Maybe I could send my brother to a nice college.* The only problem was his age. At sixteen it would be impossible to join without his father's consent, so he decided to do the next best thing. He had learned to stretch the truth a little with the help of a newfound friend. George had not lied. He was *over* eighteen—that is, the number eighteen.

When the last man had signed the company roster, the recruiting office door opened, and the sergeant stepped out along with a young captain. The captain had the men lift their right hand, and George followed along, "I, George Everson, do solemnly swear that I will bear true allegiance to the United States of America, and that I will ..." George and the men continued murmuring the rest of the lines and repeating everything the captain was saying. All solemnly swore to bear true allegiance to the United States of America. As swiftly as he had stepped out on the porch, the captain turned on his heels and went back in the building. The sergeant gathered the men around closer. "Listen up for your name as I give out your assignments." He went through some A's and got to "Baker, William. F Company." He read on through the D's and finally said, "Everson, George. F Company."

"Looks like we'll be in the same company anyway," said William.

Then they headed to Palace Gardens for training.

"You ever hear of such a place, this Palace Gardens?" William said, turning to George.

"I read about camps around Baltimore, but I'm not sure," replied George.

"Guess you do a lot of reading, huh?"

"My mother's a schoolteacher, and my dad is a preacher and a farmer. Yeah, I'd say I do my share of reading."

"What sort of readin' have you done?" asked William.

"At first I was reading stories by a fellow named Ballantyne about a coral sea and one about gorillas," replied George. A small crowd of new recruits had gathered around George, listening intently as he told them all what he had read. "Later I was reading some stuff about out West, but my parents stopped any of those smaller books coming into the house because they said they were immoral influences on the youth. But I was just about to read something from a man named Hawthorne about a—"

"Never heard of them," William blurted out, suddenly switching to matters of immediate concern. "I figured we'd be in the scrap right away."

"Well, we would, but I think this might be a new outfit. The newspapers I read tell that they get to train for a while, and then they're sent into battle. Everything's from scratch. It's the companies that are already formed where you go right into the fight."

The dust began to settle in the courtyard. A tall, older sergeant stood over to the side by the porch, looking at the group and pulling on his unusually large amount of whiskers, which ran straight down both sides of his cheeks. George thought the man looked like he had been in the saddle all his life. A loud bellow came out of the sergeant's mouth, "F Company, fall in!"

The gangly boys scrambled about until there was some form of a line—all except for George, who looked confused.

"Told ya ta fall in," he said, glaring at George.

"But sir," exclaimed George, "there's nothing to fall into."

The sergeant's face reddened with rage. There were some coughs from the others trying to hold back the laughter. "So you're the *reader* in this group. I overheard ya talkin'."

"I'm an avid reader, yes, sir," replied George.

"Well, read this, Mr. Avid. *Fall in* means form a straight line," the sergeant was now shouting. "Now git in there!"

George scurried to get within an elbow's length of the next man. The courtyard dirt flew through the air like fine powder as the men scurried and shuffled to get in a straight line. The sergeant stepped onto a porch, walked to a railing, and leaned over, and with both hands clenched the whitewashed post.

"Name is Sergeant Blunt," he continued shouting. The words were sudden, raw, and very angry. "I'm a sergeant in the US Army. You refer to me as *Sergeant*. You don't call me *sir*. That there title is reserved for officers. We're gonna teach ya to march and make soldiers outa ya." Then Sergeant Blunt continued, "One more thing—ya won't be needin' nuthin' for the next few weeks. We give ya rifles and bullets. If ya got any of those on ya, give 'em up now."

Deposited on the ground in front of Sergeant Blunt were one old musket, two flintlocks, seven balls, and two pistols. One older man next to George whispered, "He ain't no good'n to make an enemy of. He's mean, and he thinks he's another General Burnside, all proper glory 'n all."

"Land sakes, he's got to be over forty," George continued. "I thought everyone voted on who was sergeant."

"Maybe so, but that there sergeant is already been a hero," said the man next to George. "I hear tell he's a real scrapper and tore up a whole lotta Rebs in the Races at Phillipi in Virginia. He knows his stuff. His name is Sergeant Blunt. Ya can bet he'll be lookin' fer ya. And he's been in a heap more scraps, including the Battle of Manassas. He ain't fit just Johnny Reb to get them stripes."

"But—" George started.

"Not another word," continued the man. "You need to shut pan and sing small. No more words to him."

Men came from all over. *Fit* meant to fight, and he knew he was no match for this big sergeant. As they turned to march, George thought about the home he had left. He thought about his sister, Sarah, his brother, John, and his parents. He reminisced on his long train ride from Kellogsville to Annapolis, and all he had in his pocket was a dollar and two three-cent pieces. He would miss school, but most of his friends and cousins were on the same road as him. His father had taught him that once he started something, there was no turning back. And so his home was the army for the next two years.

Chapter 2

Palace Gardens

One by one, they funneled down the long rows of tents—one row of tents for one company, one tent for two to six recruits. Each side housed twelve tents with a straight, narrow path down the middle keeping each company within its boundaries. Posted at each end was a sign disclosing the chain of command and the person who was in charge of each level. Sergeant Blunt, still red from screaming, continued to bellow at the recruits. "You boys are gonna learn what a chain of command is and what it means to break that chain."

One of the recruits who dared utter a confused "What?" got the full that impact of Sergeant Blunt in his face.

"What that means, boy, is ya see me first 'fore you even think about talking to any one higher than me," said Sergeant Blunt, still in front of the recruit. He turned to the others and continued, "You are in in Company F ... and we got us about a hundred men. Captain Corey is your commanding officer. We got us ten companies in this here Fifty-first New York under Colonel Ferrero. He's got about a thousand men in this regiment. And then you got the brigade with Brigadier General Reno in charge of four regiments. And then we got us General Ambrose Burnside, the division commander, and he's got twelve thousand men. Learn this chain. Now pick a tent and stow your stuff.

George took a corner, leaving William the one toward the front of the tent. They had been issued a blanket, tin cup, plate, knife, fork, and spoon, and they stored that little bit of equipment by their feet in small sacks. Their clothing consisted of government-issue black shoes, wool pants, suspenders, white shirt, blouse with brass buttons, and hat.

"We got here late for the party, and we got us a bunch of tents all lined up," remarked William. I hear tell some fellers got barracks with bunks, and inside they look like a bowling alley. My grandfather used to play ninepin in the back streets. He said they outlawed the game 'cause of gambling. Nowadays it's tenpin. Reckon they think that stops the bettin'. Used ta make me some money at it. Not a whole lot though."

"You gambled at bowling?" quizzed George.

"Sure! I bet on most anything as long as it's a sure win," said William.

"Well, it kinda reminds me of those long furrows I plowed," said George. "Looks like these tents go from sunup to sundown just like my plowing used to." Then he thought of the sweat and aching muscles day in and day out for seven days a week. He realized even more his decision to join the army was right. He was free, and his family could use the money.

Getting acquainted and finding out why others had joined was the next order of business. Most had joined for the same reason George had—to get away from the farm.

"I joined 'cause I didn't want ta miss out," said a young blond man with a front tooth missing. "My pa got to skirmish in Mexico in '46 right after I was born. Now it's my turn."

Another recruit spoke out, "I hear them rebels is mean, and if they take over, they'll kill my family and do horrible things to my sisters." George noticed the massive amount of freckles on this short, red-haired man and reminisced about his own brother and sisters.

"Well, my old man was gonna put me to work in a factory, so I just hightailed it outta the city and joined," another young man said in a condescending manner as he fumbled with the dice in his pocket. *A hustler*, George thought.

"My family needed the money. Times have been tough," confessed another as he rubbed his hand through his matted black hair. There was a rope where a belt should be holding up his tattered pants.

George felt he could relate to the last idea. Most of these boys averaged eighteen years of age. At the far end of his tent row, he suddenly heard a loud yell and the word *cousin*.

Two young men swiftly approached, and the older one spoke, "I'm John, and this here's my brother, Lorenzo. We're the Maybrees, your cousins." John was a little taller than Lorenzo, both with long black hair and hazel eyes. They were thin, but they were ready for any action. "We got in yesterday. They started drilling us the first hour."

From the opposite end of the tent row came a booming voice. "Boys! This here's your new home," Sergeant Blunt said sarcastically. "Tomorrow right after reveille, ya drill. Tonight ya kin rest."

Murmurs came from some of the younger men. "What did he say?" they whispered in disbelief.

As if he knew what they were asking, Sergeant Blunt kept talking as he explained. "For those of ya that're new to army life, those are bugle calls. Ya got one for gittin' up. That'd be reveille. Ya got one for tellin' ya to get ready for bed or candle lightin' time is over—tattoo. And ya got a real pretty one," he continued cynically, "for tellin' ya to go to sleep—taps."

Sergeant Blunt and two other men, both corporals, walked with him up and down the row of tents as he talked, scrutinizing each recruit as if he were looking for something in particular. "Rifles will be issued later along with ammunition and such." Stopping in front of George, Sergeant Blunt scowled as he continued his reception talk. "When I tell ya ta fall in, that means git out in front of the building and stand at attention in a straight line." His gaze fixed on George's face. "Understand, Mr. Avid Reader?" The hot breath of hostility was strong as the sergeant seemed to peer down, towering above George's almost six-foot frame. The man's stature was solid, and the highly polished brass buttons seemed to radiate the mass even more.

"Yes, sir," murmured George.

"It's 'yes, *Sergeant*,' boy. You call officers sir. Understand?" Blunt jeered.

"Yes, si … Sergeant," George nervously replied.

The old man's voice became a whisper as he spoke into George's face. "I know ya ain't eighteen, boy. Ya wanted in this mess, but I don't think yore fancy reading can help. You won't last."

Blunt turned to the others and roared, "Ya got a sleeping area. Stick to it fer now. You'll need yore rest. Maybe if yer lucky, ya can get a mattress from town. Won't get much sleep after this, no how." He turned sharply on his heel and marched out followed by the two corporals.

John turned to George and said, "You'd better watch your step. You didn't make a friend with that one."

"He's been out for me since I joined," said George. "I can't figure out why he hates me so."

"Could be 'cause you can read and he cain't," came a voice from an older recruit. "But he don't know we know that. It's the Sergeant's secret."

If it's a secret, how does this man know it? thought George, trying to look away from the lean, older man who just made the statement.

George turned and gazed out a tent door at the now moonlit field. Row after row of the huge log tents identical to the one he was in stretched out like a city. He could make out an attempt of small furrows around some of the tents to drain off the rains. He could make out a few men, some in uniform, rustling by the side of the building and smoking. By the gestures of their arms, he concluded they were playing a form of dice. Turning to William, George's closest expert to gambling, he asked what they might be doing.

"Probably chuck-a-luck, a sort played with three dice," answered William. One of the men suddenly halted the game, and they broke up to go inside. A sentry walked by shortly after. Tomorrow was coming too soon. A lonely, disturbing, but beautiful tune filled the air as the bugle sounded taps.

Chapter 3

The Awakening

George stirred and looked at the ceiling with wide eyes as he thought, *How could the same bugle that had sounded so peaceful last night be so ruthless? The sun isn't even up.* The sound vibrated the air with a rapid "It's-time-to-get-up. It's-time-to-get-up. It's- time-to-get-up-in-the mo-orning!"

Dust rose as feet shuffled, and there was a commotion of scrambling men fighting their way to the freshly dug ditch latrine in the back. George looked around and saw that at least two blankets hadn't been slept in the night before.

"Deserters," said William. "I guess Sergeant Blunt's speech got to 'em."

"What happens if they're caught?" George asked.

"More'n likely they be shot," the old recruit from last night piped in. "From what I hear, it's a gruesome sight to behold. They gotta drag their own coffin out with 'em and stand by it while the whole company looks on. Or they could be real lenient and have them ride the pole for a couple of days."

"Ride the pole?" quizzed George.

"That's where you have to straddle a pole like a horse and sit there sometimes for days."

"That doesn't sound so bad."

"Oh, but it is," the old recruit responded. "It hurts something awful after a bit. I seen some that couldn't walk for days after that punishment."

"Why don't they just throw them in jail?" asked George.

"Simple. They ain't got no calaboose for the army on such short notice."

George discovered the old recruit's name was Jacob Penny. He'd served with the militia back in New York. Jacob was about the same age as Sergeant Blunt, but didn't have the belly or the same mountainous physique. His hair was darker and longer, but his face was clean-shaven.

The bugle sounded again with a different call. The men emptied the tents hurriedly and ran outside to stand in front. Over the next few weeks, this routine of jumping different ways to different calls of the bugle would become second nature for George. There were bugle sounds for meals, flag raising, flag lowering, retreat, charge, and formation. There was even a bugle call for mail. If they were not drilling, they were sitting around, playing cards, or reading letters from home.

Sergeant Blunt drilled them early each morning. This morning was different. They had been marched to a building, and the camp was going to issue them rifles. "This is a US Army Springfield rifle," he bellowed out to them from a makeshift crate he was standing on. "It costs fourteen dollars and ninety-eight cents and is accurate up to three hundred yards." Whispers came from the ranks, and Sergeant Blunt continued, "If yore lucky and you get seasoned, you can get two shots a minute off."

"What's that thing shoot?" muttered   someone so low that George could barely hear him. Somehow, Sergeant Blunt sensed the question.

"This thing shoots a mini ball packed in this paper pouch with its own supply of powder," he explained. "Someone got confused 'cause this thing is named after some French feller named Ma'nay. Ain't nothing mini bout it."

"These're as big as my thumb," George said to Jacob. "They look like they'd tear a wall off a barn."

Sergeant Blunt continued the demonstration. "First thing after you tear open the paper cartridge is pour the powder down the barrel," and Blunt did just that. "Then push in the bullet with yore thumb like so." Blunt stuck the bullet on top of the barrel and pushed the large mini ball down a bit. "After that, ya draw yore ramrod out and push the bullet down into the barrel."

"Pretty simple so far," someone whispered again.

"Now," Sergeant Blunt went on, "ya gotta pull the hammer back and then put this little percussion cap on. That's for when ya let it slam down it makes a spark and lights the powder inside, making the bullet fly." As he explained, he put the percussion cap on his rifle. Then he aimed it down range and fired, shocking anyone who was trying to slumber because of the loudness.

George, a crack shot with a musket back home, became a sharpshooter on the rifle range. "There's something you should know about war," Jacob said. "It gives them inventors a chance to play, and whoever comes up with the meanest weapon gets the prize."

"But," George insisted, "this thing looks like something from a cannon instead of a rifle barrel. It's twice the size of anything I've ever used for hunting, and it's hallowed out somewhat. It's gonna spread when it hits something. Things an inch long at least and half inch round. Maybe they want us to use these bayonets."

"Oh, no!" Jacob lurched as though he'd been hit, his dark eyes slightly stirred to displeasure. "You don't do something to them that you don't want done to you. No one wants to die like that, so we don't use them things unless we really have to. We start to use bayonets, then the Rebs will too."

"Besides," someone else added, "it's too close and personal. Somebody may have kin on the other side."

"And one more thing," William said and laughed. "It's a candle holder. What am I gonna do for my card game at night?"

George pondered over this and other things he thought were a little peculiar about the army's way of doing things. He wasn't the only one who questioned things. Early one morning during drill, John Maybrees turned to Sergeant Blunt and said, "Sergeant, why don't we quit all this foolishness and just go over to the Sutler and get something to eat?"

The Sutler was always behind all the camps following them everywhere with high prices. There was one merchant per regiment appointed by the government to supply troops with pastries, tobacco, and other things. Some sold goods on credit and deducted the cost from their pay.

Sergeant Blunt was quiet for a second, and then he turned to one of his corporals. "Take this young coot out and drill him until he drops." With a smirk on his face, he looked directly at George and called to the corporal, "Take this one with you too." He dismissed the rest of the company. George started to mumble something but thought better of it. He was learning that this sergeant could do and get away with many things. For three hours George and his cousin had managed to drill.

It was dark when they finally entered the barracks. William and Jacob met George.

"He's still got it in for you," Jacob observed. "I think he was hoping you'd run off so's he could shoot yuh."

"I'm not giving in," exclaimed George. "But I've been thinking. I should get me a pistol."

"Now hold on," Jacob blurted. "You got some crazy notion to try to shoot the Sarge?"

"No!" George exclaimed. "I had time to think out there today on the drill field after rifle practice. Those Springfield rifles are nice, but I can only get off about two rounds a minute. It takes too long to tear open the paper cartridge, pour powder down the barrel, ram it all in, and put the cap under the hammer."

"You're starting to sound like one of them inventors I was telling you about," said Jacob. "But even so, they don't look too kindly on enlisted havin' pistols."

"I'm gonna get me one anyway."

"You think Sergeant Blunt's got it in for you now. Wait 'til he finds you with a pistol," Jacob exhaled a low whistle. Fully dressed except for his blouse and hat, George fell into his bunk as the sound of taps filled the night air. According to Jacob, it was easier to sleep with clothes on. It made it that much easier in the morning when everyone had to rush out to formation. George had to agree with that. That, and there was absolutely no privacy.

Another week had passed and still the company drilled and practiced on the rifle range. They were becoming "seasoned" or "aged," as Sergeant Blunt told them. Jacob had become an orderly sergeant taking care of sick call and other small company duties—a promotion based on his previous experience—and the men looked up to him. He did not have quite the same command as Sergeant Blunt, and his stripes were of a different color. For a full week, George had been a frequent visitor to Jacob's sick call because of bad food. In fact, George was almost sent home because of the visits.

George was due for guard duty that came around every four weeks. The drizzle had not let up for two days. Wetness made the tents stifle with fetid odors. George, exhausted after his last shift on guard, walked over to his blanket. There, Sergeant Blunt, who had entered the tent area for the morning inspection, confronted him.

"Ya had yore two on and four off for twenty-four hours. But that ain't enough, Private Everson," Blunt sneered. "Report back to the guard house."

George was dumbfounded. Something was wrong. Wearily, he packed up his rifle. Sergeant Blunt was commanding him to walk another day of guard duty. George decided to stop on the way to his post and talk to Jacob.

"Jacob, Sergeant Blunt has me walking guard again," George said. "That's a pretty long stretch. Can he do that?"

"According to regulations, no," Jacob said. "But who's gonna stop him? And how?"

"Since you're a sergeant too, I thought you might talk to him," George said.

Both of them walked over to the headquarters where Sergeant Blunt was staying. Jacob had a copy of the regulations with him. It was his new job to post rules and regulations. He knew that Sergeant Blunt was not that good of a reader or could not read, so he also had them with him just in case there was a disagreement. Jacob had George stand outside and away from the tent to make it appear he was out of hearing distance.

"Sergeant Blunt," Jacob commenced, "Private Everson has done his guard duty time according to regulations."

Hissing his words out, Blunt squared off, "Don't need nobody to quote me regulations! I can read good as any man."

Jacob had said Blunt could not read. Any word now would be calling Blunt a liar. George kept quiet and a few paces back, sensing that any moment this huge bulk of a man might charge into both of them, smash them down, and get away with it.

"Sergeant Blunt," Jacob continued, trying to keep the calm, "there's gotta be some mistake."

"Thank you, Sergeant Penny," Blunt hissed. "Consider it corrected. Dismissed. Botha ya."

Jacob and George both did a sharp about-face and marched off smartly. "Now he'll have a real mean grudge against both us," said Jacob.

"I'm sorry," George said. "I didn't mean for you to get your neck in a noose."

"He won't bother me. I know some things about him that keeps me ahead." George wondered what they were, but he didn't ask. It was starting to get cold, and rumors were flying through the air now that they were becoming seasoned soldiers. "By the way, you got a letter today at mail call while you wuz on guard duty." The letter was six weeks old, and that afternoon George decided he'd better write a quick return letter to his family.

Palace Gardens—October 20, 1861

Dear Father, Mother, Sisters, and Brother,

Mother, you wanted I should write how I was getting along. Now I will tell you how it is. I have not forgotten you. As for being homesick, I was a little homesick once, and I think I had reasons for it. I was sick as I was any time last winter and could not get around. Lying around day after day will make a fellow think of home, but now I am well and not homesick at all.

I am enjoying myself better than if I were at home. Here something is going on all the time, such as singing and all kinds of tricks and playing cards, but I have nothing to do with cards. George and Lorenzo Maybrees are in the same company that I am. We are good friends for all that I know of. We begin to look like soldiers now, for we got our overcoats, knapsacks, canteens, guns, cartridge boxes, and belts. We are aged, and Wednesday morning we start for the capitol of Maryland to drill a short time. And then we go to Washington. Now this may not be true, but it came from good quarters.

Mother, you need not send anything to me for I might not get it. As far as our chaplain's name, I can't find out what it is. But he is a Methodist, and I guess a pretty good sort of man as far as I know.

Father, you thought that I would have a hard time on guard, but I do not, for I have just been on guard, and my turn comes again in four weeks. Then it is two hours on and four hours off, and so you see, we do not have it very hard.

As for my coming home, I never said I was coming home, and I don't see what made anyone think so.

When I was sick, our orderly sergeant told me if I didn't get better before a great while that I would have to go to the hospital or get a discharge. But now I don't want one. Now I am well.

But I cannot write anymore at present, but if we leave here, I will write as soon as we stop. You need not answer this. So good-bye.

George W. Everson

Chapter 4

Camp Burnside

Canvas mounds sprawled out for acres, and uniformed ants rushed about. Some had nicknamed the place "tent city," which was now headquarters for the Fifty-first Regiment and Company F. The name of the place appeared to be the idea of the new first sergeant, Sergeant Blunt. The one hundred men of Company F were encamped near the ten other companies by a small stream where they did their washing, cleaning, bathing, and drinking. Most days were now measured by mealtimes. George's eating utensils were his tin dipper, tin plate, knife, fork, and spoon.

"Where do we put this eating stuff?" George asked one day to no one in particular in the tent

"I just throw 'em under my blanket," was one answer.

"I mean, where do we clean them?"

"Just scrape 'em, George. You're gonna have to use 'em again anyhow."

"But," insisted George, "my knife is so dirty it's turning black."

"That's easy," said William, "just stick it in the ground a few times. Cleans up nice and shiny."

"Sometimes I just use leaves to clean out my plate. Works real good," came another answer.

Inspections were more frequent now. Cleaning the area, sweeping out the tents, and general police call were the order of the day every day. Thanksgiving had passed on the road, and now Christmas was coming. Inspection time was drawing near, and George Everson had not cleaned his rifle. Fearing his first sergeant would get angry, he told him, "Jed Crampton was chasing a pig for the regimental cook. He tore into our area and knocked our rifles into the dirt just prior to inspection." Sergeant Blunt's eyes squinted, and a question started to form on his lips and then vanish. George's bluff seemed to pay off for now. However, he pondered why Blunt had not pursued the matter. Blunt did not appreciate the fact the officers ate better than the enlisted men did, and where else would the pig go but to the officers' mess tent. George's cousin Lorenzo Maybees from the same outfit but housed a few tents away thought that sounded very peculiar. When Lorenzo saw Jed, he prodded him about the clumsy act.

Jed felt blamed for the dirty rifles, so he decided to tell a whopper of his own. "What George didn't tell ya was them rifles was dirty 'cause he was afraid to tell his first sergeant that he and several fellows were in a brawl yesterday in the company area and didn't get 'round to cleanin' them rifles."

Lorenzo had a knack for building yarns and starting gossip. That night he saw his best friend, Bill, from Company C. "Did ya hear about the big brawl in Company F yesterday?" Lorenzo asked. "They ripped the place up."

Bill told his company's first sergeant, "I heard there was a brawl over at Company F yesterday. About twenty men, including one of ours, who'd gone over to deliver some reports."

"Well, why didn't I hear about any of this?" his first sergeant bellowed. The first sergeant of Company C became very concerned, so he decided to tell his adjutant, Lieutenant Colfax. They decided to call on Company F the next day to discuss the matter. By now, the story was that "close to fifty men had a brawl between companies while several noncoms stood around and did nothing!"

Rumors flew like whirlwinds. Not remembering a fight, some believed the fight must have happened at the nearby Sutler, the civilian store that followed regiments anywhere they went, supplying food and other assorted sundries. That evening the talk in all the camps was that somewhere around a hundred boys from two different regiments had a huge fight at Sutler's and some fellows got taken to the calaboose.

In about a week, stories about fights between companies hit the newspapers, and General Ambrose E. Burnside, commanding the army in that area, decided to take action. The Sutler would be off limits for three weeks. While George stared at the "off limits" sign posted near the traveling store, he couldn't imagine that it was his lie about the rifle that had caused all this. No more molasses cakes or cookies for twenty-five cents. Then there were the inspections. The Sutler, accompanied by a detachment of men, would fling things about in each tent, looking for stolen goods. With a sigh, George's only thoughts now were to finish cleaning his rifle for the next inspection and the fantasy that Sergeant Blunt had somehow known this would happen. That's why he didn't say anything about the little white lie.

William had other plans for George. There was to be a card game tonight, and the stakes were high. Against all his parents' teaching, against all his better judgment, George was swayed by William's smooth city angle that he could beat the odds. He was still insisting *no* when the final blow came from William. "George," William challenged, "I double-dog dare ya."

Idle time is something a soldier fears more than battle. It gives a person too much of a chance to think about what is going to happen rather than what is happening. After all the drilling, all the target practice, all the cleaning up, and all the inspections, a soldier finds ways to fill his time. Usually it's with alcohol. The Fifty-first was fast becoming a large unit with a questionable reputation. Idle time brings gossip. Rumors were always spreading. One night as George's tent was sitting around a candle, William exclaimed he had heard the whole brigade was pulling out to go to Fortress Monroe.

"Do you reckon we're gonna see some fighting soon?" asked George.

"Well," another soldier said, "I heard we were gonna be stuck here all winter and the rest of the regiment was pulling out."

"Well," another one chortled, "I suppose the town got enough of the Fifty-first filling up the calaboose with our rowdy boys and the boozin' that they might have voted we be the ones to pull out."

The conversation soon died down, and the thoughts idled toward ways to cure the boredom without the alcohol or the town. With the help of William, George found time for cards.

"Looka here, George," William said, "just take my signals. When I drop my hand, you fold too."

"That's cheating," exclaimed George.

"No, that's learning."

George's hands were shaking as they entered the tent. Four others were sitting cross-legged around an overturned empty crate. Soldiers watching crowded in behind them—a total of ten men in a small tent. The older one was lean with a small beard, and he spoke first. "Well, William, I hear yor pretty good with cards. Now we're gonna find out if that ain't just bull." George knew this was the new slang going around camp for lying.

George found himself next to William. William's plan was coming together. They made introductions, and George learned the man with the beard running the show was Jake Reynolds. His hands were fast. The cards flew across the makeshift table and landed perfectly in front of their holders. Stakes were low at first, only a three-cent piece to get in or stay in. They soon became higher. George whispered to William, "There must be near ten dollars in the middle of the table."

Jake's harsh tone cut through the air, "Ya don't talk to no one at the table unless yor bettin', and ya don't count the kitty. It's bad luck!" Jake's luck was running out, and he was down quite a bit. William had a large pile of coins in front of him. Jake would peer at George and then William through his gunmetal-colored eyes. Then slowly, he would bet. Like the rest of the group, George was holding his own. He had about the same amount he had started with. William would send his signals, and George would start squirming, shifting, and beads of sweat would roll down his forehead. The night was cold, but the inside of the crowded tent became stifling with body odor and heat. George was holding four jacks and a queen. He was trying to keep calm, remembering what William had told him, "No matter what you're holding, don't show no emotions." William had been dealing. Inside George questioned whether William had intentionally dealt him this particular hand. The betting was finished except for Jake. Then it happened. Jake drew a pistol out of his jacket.

———

"Whoa!" William shouted. "There's no need for that!" At the same time, two other men dashed for the tent flap to get out. George's thoughts of back home flashed through his head. *All this drilling and I'm going to get killed in a ridiculous card game. Keep your mouth shut, stay calm, and show no emotions,* echoed through George's head. William's instructions. George knew they had been caught. Now they would pay!

Slowly, Jake set the pistol on the table. "This here is worth nine dollars," he said. "Ima bettin' this. And I call."

George knew this meant everyone had to show his hand now or get out of this game. William didn't fold. George followed as told. All of them put their cards on the table slowly, and George's hand took the pot. They dealt several more hands, but George's luck had run out. At the end of the night, he had no money, only a nine-dollar pistol.

George hefted the pistol in his hand and felt it repeatedly. "It's a fine gun," he told William on the way back to their camp. "It holds six shots and is short like blazes. But how will I explain it to my parents?"

"Just tell them you're gonna buy one and that everyone has one," William said.

"Sergeant Blunt will be after this," George continued.

"I've heard his speech. No soldier should have anything 'cept what's issued. We ain't got time or space for extras."

"But I don't want to get caught in battle without something if I drop my rifle," George said.

"It's small enough," William replied. "You should be able to hide it easily."

That night and over the next few nights, George wrote his parents again.

Headquarters Annapolis—51 Regt.

Co. F

Camp Burnside—Dec. 20, 1861

Dear Father, Brother, Sisters,

We have fine weather here so far. No snow and the coloreds husking corn for you don't see a white man work any here. I should like to have you here this forenoon to the review. There was about 1,200, 1,400 men reviewed by Gen. Burnside. Now I tell you it made quite a show all armed and equipped. Mother, I talk of buying a revolver. It is something that everyone needs, and a great many have them. That Reynolds that I told you about has one and wants to sell it for he wants a larger one. This is not very small but common size and short like blazes. He will let me have it for nine dollars and trust me till payday, which is in three weeks.

Father, Mother, you think that I am not enjoying myself, but to tell the truth, I am taking comfort, have easy times, plenty of eat, and John, as I say, if I stayed at home, I could have laid in bed till noon. I have plenty of sleep here, and without the trouble of undressing when I go to bed, for I only take off my cap, coat, and shoes. So you can see we have it easy.

Father, I wish you were here with your old rifle. I would like to shoot at a mark with my old musket. A hundred yards I shot three times the other day and hit the mark. I suppose we shall leave here in a week or two perhaps to go to South Carolina, but I mistrust by what I have heard that we will go down on the Potomac.

Dec. 21, 1861

Mother, we expect to be paid off in a short time, and then we will leave this place. And it may be six months before we are paid again, and if you can get along without me sending some wages home. Father,

I wish you had one of my blankets for a horse blanket, for I have one States blanket and one United States, two rubber blankets. One I bought and the other the citizens of New York City gave to us.

John, I will write a few lines to you. What do the young folks say about me? I want you should write what you study, and I advise you to study geography. Though you may think you are well enough in that branch, you are mistaken, and you will find out if you ever undertake to travel alone.

Sarah and Jane, I suppose you go to school every day this winter, and I hope you learn very fast. And if you only try to attend to your books you can learn.

Dec. 22, 1861

Dear parents,

I have just tore this letter open to let you know we received that box this morning and was glad to get it. We shall keep it all to ourselves except one roll of butter, which I will give to our orderly sergeant, for he is a fine fellow and he will give me any favor I ask of him. We can't get butter here as you sent. Butter is thirty cents a pound and poor at that. Ccheese

is fifteen cents, but we can get a good meal at our

Suttlers any time a day for twenty-five cents.

Write soon.

—George W. Everson

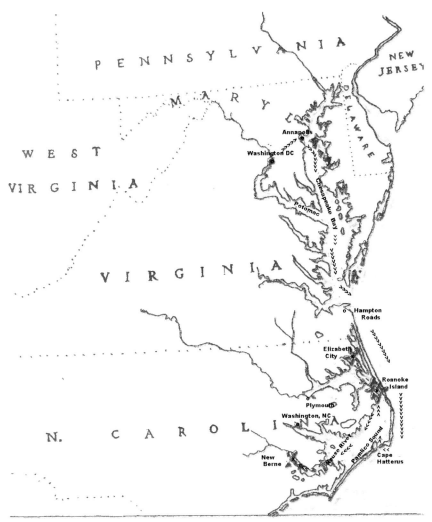

PENNSYLVANIA

NEW JERSEY

M A R Y L

WEST

VIRGINIA

Annapolis

Washington DC

DELAWARE

Chesapeake Bay

Potomac

V I R G I N I A

o Hampton
Roads

Elizabeth
City

Roanoke
Island

Plymouth

Washington, NC

N.   C A R O L I

Pamlico Sound

Neuse River

New
Berne

Cape
Hatterus

Ships lost: 3
Lives Lost: 12+/-   Transported: 15,000 men
Horses Lost: 100

Chapter 5

Cape Hatteras

Folding back the tent flaps and clamoring to get into ranks for reveille, the boys from F Company found two inches of snow and more coming as fast as possible. Some men were still staggering from last night after the brigade commander, Colonel Ferrero, told them, "Be boys tonight, for we are going to battle." The colonel was a trim, dapper, black-haired little man, something of a dandy in his dress, and he laughed for a while and became real loud, "Yes, by God! We are going to do battle."

George turned to William. "You look a little peaked, William. Ain't you excited?"

"George! There's two inches of snow on the ground. It's still coming down, and in thirty minutes we have to have our knapsacks packed and on the road to Annapolis to board some ship. How do you find that exciting?"

After two days of marching, the Fifty-first was finally at the landing in Annapolis. The regiment was split between two steamers, the *Lancer* and the *Pioneer*. Anchored nearby were converted barges, ferryboats, sailing vessels, and tugs. One of the boys commented that it looked like New York Harbor. Added to the other boats were gunboats, sloops, ocean steamers and river steamers.

"A real motley fleet for fifteen thousand troops," exclaimed William. "Some of these old tubs don't look like they could float." One day passed, and the troops were still being loaded on the boats.

Jacob was now with George and William, telling them all the details of the loading procedures. "I hear-tell that there was some reluctance from one small craft," Jacob said. "They were convinced it would sink."

Throughout the regiments, some men had traded the water in their canteens for whiskey. By nightfall, hundreds of them were drunk, clamoring around the loading platforms and planks. Whiskey was confiscated from packages, but a few of the seasoned veterans would smuggle in bottles stuffed in cooked turkeys during the Christmas season. By the time F Company arrived, the whiskey had begun to exhibit its affects, and a fight started. Then pandemonium broke out between the two companies, and a regular old-fashioned free fight went on for about half an hour.

Several men from different companies tried to take over the gangplanks of the various boats and challenge all who came aboard by asking for a password. George was challenged and passed. The small group challenged another young man coming up the gangplank. Jacob looked at George. "Here's trouble. This one is a pie eater from

D Company. What we call country boys," Jacob explained. They knocked the man down, and another fight broke out. George hadn't realized there was such dislike between country and city boys. This was all because of whiskey.

The next morning they made sail, and the "Burnside Expedition," which is what they called it now, arrived at Fort Monroe, Virginia, two days later at about 2:00 p.m. When the fog lifted, George counted paddle-wheel steamers, sailing boats, propeller-driven steamers, canal boats, surfboats, and launches. Some would carry a thousand men; other small ones would only carry a hundred men. Jacob Penny had said there were some twenty thousand or so men on this expedition under General Burnside, and they were going to Cape Hatteras, all eighty vessels.

"We're packed in here like herrings," said Jacob, "and no one dares to leave their area of one foot by one foot of wooden plank for fear of losing their space."

"They leave us on here much longer, and I can lick them Rebs all by myself," said George. They were saving a spot for William, who had gone above again to "feed the fish" as Jacob said. Most of the boys were sick. The ocean had turned into rolling hills of billows the day they had left Fort Monroe, swallowing boats only to be spit back up and rolled about like apples bobbing in a barrel. Men were knocked about like rag dolls. "It's enough to make a person think over his past life," George exclaimed to no one in particular. This raging storm began the night after passing Cape Henry just one day out.

George watched with pleasure as even Sergeant Blunt, who stood like a rock on shore, tumbled about as if something finally had control over him. Pleasure soon turned to agony as George himself felt the tumbling inside. George, William, and Jacob had crawled to the nearest pole to hang on for fear of being tossed overboard or being trapped below. Each huge wave pounded the boats, smashing over the side and pouring into decks below. Suddenly, they heard someone a shout, "Man overboard," through the deafening roar of the furious sea. George turned to check on his comrades.

"I see him," Jacob hollered. "It's that new boy."

Edging toward the side of the boat, Jacob put his hand out toward the youth flailing in the choppy waters when another sudden wave pushed Jacob back. George was closest now. Each billow would raise the boat and then lower it so the side would touch the water. Crawling on his stomach, he extended his arm over the side. Then he felt the stabbing sensation in his back. His pistol jarred loose. The boy's hand was closer, just a few more inches. Then George felt behind to straighten the pistol he had hidden in his trousers in the small of his back. Reaching his hand around to fix the pistol, he lost sight of the boy's hand. Yelling at the top of his voice, George frantically searched for any sign of a bobbing head or extending hand. The sea had swallowed the young boy. *My God, what have I done?* thought George. He didn't want to lose his pistol, but the price had already cost a life. He lay there with tears in his eyes, tears driven away by the salty seawater smashing into his face. He had one last vision of the desperate look in the young boy's eyes as he reached for George, and George had pulled back his own hand to fix the pistol.

"You done all you could, boy," Jacob shouted. "You should be proud."

Angry, frustrated thoughts flowed in George's head. *Proud! How can I be proud? All I could think about was my pistol.* Now William was patting him on the shoulder as well. The night was long, and the sea kept battering them. Eighty vessels had battled the enraged sea. On January 13, the ragtag fleet was forced to anchor at Hatteras Inlet because of heavy fog. Most of the men were still seasick and haggard from the journey. Bleary-eyed troops watched as warships of the North Atlantic Blockading Squadron materialized out of the fog like ghosts. Jacob counted twenty. He later learned that some of the vessels on this expedition had been carried out to sea. Others had been driven ashore, and a total of five had been wrecked. The young boy wasn't the only one lost. About four hundred men were unaccounted for, gone.

Despite all the delays and storms, they were to start inward to Pamlico Sound so they could unload troops. The sea was still angry and tossing the boats around as they tried to maneuver through the inlet.

"We can't get through," said Jacob, who had been talking to sailors and bringing information back to George and the others.

"It seems we need eight feet of water to pass through, but we only find six."

"Are we stuck for good, or do we turn back?" asked George.

"Neither," said Jacob.

"But you said we couldn't get through," exclaimed William.

"It's kinda hard to explain," continued Jacob. "But we're in for a lot of work."

They found out soon enough. Sergeant Blunt chose George for one of the rowing details. All the time George felt the glaring, beady eyes of Sergeant Blunt peer into his soul as if he knew exactly what had happened the night the sea had taken the young boy, screaming at George, *It's your fault!*

"Private Everson," Blunt said, "you report to that there crew over yonder, and when the steamer runs aground, row that anchor out and drop it."

"First Sergeant," George questioned, "if they run aground, won't that tear the bottom out?"

"Do it, boy!" Blunt commanded.

One of the sailors explained to George that running aground during low tide would strand the steamer only until the next ebb tide washed the sand from underneath the boat. Then they could move a little farther up into the sound.

As soon as low tide approached, George watched as steamers purposely ran themselves aground on the bar that blocked the inlet. Then George and others, mostly sailors, would row out in small boats carrying the anchors. When the ships were firmly anchored on the bar, the swift-running ebb tides washed the sand from under them. As soon as the ships were afloat, crews repeated the process. This process went on for two weeks. All the while, the storm still raged. Ships still bobbed about like apples. Some would collide with one another.

On one particular day, two army officers from another company were alongside George's boat. Their surfboat was to take the anchor out as the others, lay it, and row back. The waters were choppy, and the rowing difficult. Unexpectedly, their surfboat capsized on one of the sandbars. Fluttering about in the choppy waters, the two officers went down, never to be seen again. The sea had swallowed them as it did the young boy that George let slip. Finally, on January 26, the channel was open, and by February 4, the entire fleet lay at anchor in Pamlico Sound. Three more vessels had been lost. It seemed to George that this formidable natural foe was depleting the expedition before it had a chance to fight the Rebs.

They had endured the discomforts and dangers of midwinter in the North Atlantic. Jacob told George and William, "If we can fight nature, we can fight anything." There was no fear left, and 2,500 Johnny Rebs on one little island against twenty thousand troops would be no match.

That night George composed another letter to his parents.

Fifty-first NYV

Company F

Annapolis

I am idle this afternoon. I will give you a short sketch of our voyage under Gen. Burnside to Fortress Monroe and thence to Cape Hatteras.

Jan. 4, we were ordered out when we mistrusted something and fell in double quick time to our parade grounds and fired a few blank cartridges and then closed in mass. Our colonel rides up and says we strike tents at half past seven with four days' ration, knapsacks packed. March to Annapolis thence on board the vessels.

Jan. 5, we marched to Annapolis and went aboard the vessels. Nothing more transpired that day or that is worth quoting.

Jan. 8, hoisted anchor and made sail. Sailed till one o'clock ... the next morning and were overtaken by a heavy fog and dropped anchor and laid there till the next morning. Made sail and arrived at Fortress Monroe about 2:00 p.m.

Jan. 10, at dusk made sail and passed Cape Hatteras the morning of the twelfth and arrived at Hatteras Island the same day about noon. Though it was almost calm, the bellows rolled, and the boat rocked so a person could not stand up. And it was well passed as we did for that night an awful storm arose, and one of our vessels was lost, which was late in crossing. And the storm raged for two days.

Jan. 15, three of our gunboats went out this morning, and now we can hear them engaging some rebel batteries. And now it is about 2:00 p.m. We have started someplace, and I presume that before tomorrow we will be engaged. You will hear from me again soon if nothing happens to me.

—G. W. Everson

George didn't fondle the pistol as much anymore, turning it over and over in his hands, feeling the weight, aiming at fake targets, and then cleaning and loading it. It had lost some of its magic. Nevertheless, it was still his.

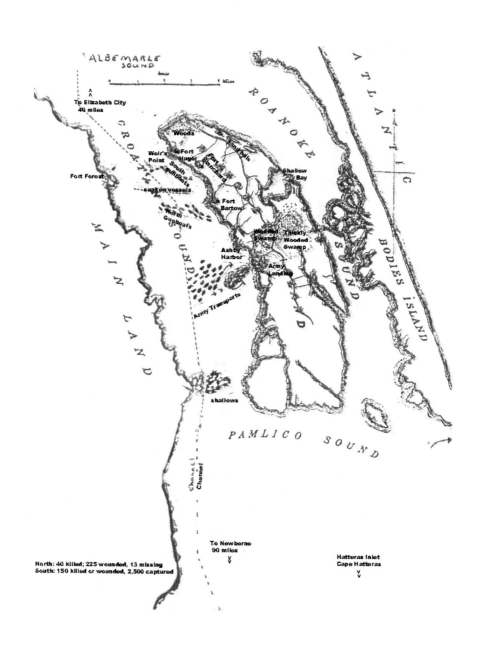

ALBEMARLE SOUND

ATLANTIC

ROANOKE

To Elizabeth City
40 miles

Woods

Fort
Huger

Weir's
Point

Fort
Blanchard

Sand Hills

Shallow
Bay

Fort Forest

South
gunboats

sunken vessels

Fort Bartow

BODIES ISLAND

North
Gunboats

Masked
Swamp

Thickly
Wooded
Swamp

MAIN

Ashby
Harbor

Army
Landing

SOUND

CROATAN

LAND

Army Transports

shallows

PAMLICO   SOUND

Channel

Channel

To Newberne
90 miles
V

North: 40 killed; 225 wounded, 13 missing
South: 150 killed or wounded, 2,500 captured

Hatteras Inlet
Cape Hatteras
V V

Chapter 6

Roanoke Island

Twenty-six days on board. They had lived in cramped quarters and tossed about like pigs in a slaughterhouse car. Some of them had to come aboard others from stranded vessels, and others were in vessels thumping for days on sandbanks under constant fear of collision. After they threw supplies and other deadweight overboard, the vessels made their way through the Hatteras Inlet to weigh anchor off the west of Roanoke Island. Thick fog had halted the attack. Weather had indeed taken a high toll from the awkward fleet. It took two more days of ships creeping in single file through the narrow channel entrance to Croatan Sound. The next day, National gunboats advanced in three columns and began to shell Fort Fartow, the principal defense on the west side of the island. The Confederate gunboats were driven off, and the fort was silenced four hours later. Finally, the call to shore came, and they disembarked. Each brigade had a light steamer with some twenty surfboats in a long line in the rear. The surfboats were filled with troops. Then as the steamer approached the shore at a rapid speed, the boats were released and speedily reached the shoreline. In less than twenty minutes, four thousand men had been set on shore, the Fifty-first among them, about two miles south of the fort that had been shelled. By midnight the entire division of twenty thousand men landed.

"I thought we would just ram the shore and keep going," exclaimed William. "They're still shooting at the boats. It's some sight to see our howitzers throwing it back at 'em."

"Kinda reminds me of the Fourth of July back home," added Jacob. "Everyone get down!" came a shout. The loud whistling came closer. *Ka-whump!* Sparks everywhere. Dust, dirt, water spray, mud. "We're six miles from that there fort," Jacob said as men began getting back up and dusting themselves off and holding their ears from the ringing. "It must've been one of ours gone awry. Dad burned idiots are shootin' short."

"Awright! Get up off yor lards," came another, much harsher shout. "We're marchin', so move it." It was Sergeant Blunt bellowing out orders and moving in and out among the men, getting them into line. He was checking out each one to see if they were hurt. It was a side of Blunt that George hadn't seen—a concerned side. Each man had his knapsack, rifle, canteen, and forty rounds of ammunition. They left the blankets and tents on board because they were so wet. They had gained twice their weight. It was usually forty pounds, but after the storm and two weeks of wet weather, the equipment was soaked. The rain started again. All night the rains pounded the men with no tents and no shelter.

The next morning the order to march came. The rain had stopped, but it was still cloudy and overcast. More rain threatened. Just to move without the element underneath them swaying was a blessing to most. Just to move freely was a blessing for others. Sergeant Blunt was again bellowing out orders to march. Moving alongside the men, he said, "Okay, boys, we got ten miles to cover. Look sharp." Each man checked his rifle, gear, and bayonet, and George reached around to check the small of his back where his pistol rested. He wanted no part of bayonet charges.

It was the middle of winter, but the humidity was stifling. "It's cold out here, and I'm still sweatin'," George complained. After a while the common sound of marching became a squishing sound. Some troops were knee-deep in mud, tromping through the marshes. The sound of clattering canteens, clicking rifles against bayonet scabbards, and the pulling effort and suction sound of feet in and out of mud was all that one could hear. There were a few dissenters with their groans and occasional quiet talk or questions, but for the most part, the hundred men marched in silence. Anything else was needless effort.

"Jacob," George said, "now that we're here, I'm not sure there's a reason for fightin' the Rebs for this island."

"We're cuttin' off their supply route. We control that, we cut down the time and get this thing over with."

"Yup," another voice from behind said, "and gettin' us on this here island means we got no place to run if the fightin' gets too hot."

"I ain't runnin' from no one," George said. "I been on that boat so long I'm mean enough to whip anything."

"You'll have that there chance soon 'nuff," came the gruff voice of Sergeant Blunt. "We're takin' the left of the fort. The Twenty-first Mass'll be takin' the right. Now get ready."

This was it. Their first charge. They had marched about half a mile along a narrow winding path through thick underbrush, marsh, and small pines. Now just six hundred yards away was the first small fortification, just a house surrounded by Rebs.

"Get down!" The first shower of bullets came buzzing overhead from the rear and the front. Blunt had them lying on their bellies to avoid both enemy and Union fire. *Buz-zzz. Hmmmm-mm.* "Sounds like great big bees with a whistle attached," said William.

Jacob hurriedly set him straight, "Those bees got a nasty sting." Five minutes felt like a lifetime facedown in the wet dirt with the buzzing overhead. Without warning, the soldier got on his feet and turned to run. *Buzz-splat!* George watched in shock as the last buzz stopped. The soldier stood there, hands twitching, legs wobbling. His head was half gone. A bloody pulp. Then he fell. William turned his head and vomited, still lying facedown.

"Charge!" Men started clambering to their feet. Rifles cocked. The smoke was like a thick blue fog. Fear turned to rage. More men fell, jolted back, twitching. Finally lying still. The frustration of thirty days of cramped quarters, fighting storms, sandbars, rain, and the sea's clutching hands, all now vented on the enemy in front of them. Daring to be hit, they were leaning into the onslaught of bullets. Jacob toppled. George stopped and plunged to his knees beside him, clutching Jacob's collar. *"No!"* George cried out. Jacob's dead eyes stared cold straight ahead, his pupils pinpointed as the life floated out of him. "Keep movin', ya fools," Sergeant Blunt shouted, herding the stragglers into some kind of formation. They had to finish the charge. George stood and aimed straight ahead. The rifle misfired. In desperation, he leaned over one of the dead men, grabbed his rifle, and fired. Any feelings of remorse had left him. Now George's only thought was to shoot as many Rebs as he could. The rage in him was a living thing. He would bite and tear the paper off the cartridge with powder and ball, pour the powder down the barrel, push the bullet in with his thumb, ram it down the barrel, pull back the hammer, put the percussion cap on, point, and shoot. Each shot took less than a minute, and he soon exhausted his forty rounds. He ripped an ammo pouch from a nearby dead Rebel soldier and continued his firing, stepping over the carcass with as little feeling as stepping over a log. Inching their way toward the small

fort, someone shouted, "Fix bayonets!" The air was so thick with gunpowder that the man next to him was barely visible. Breathing grew difficult. It began to rain again, pushing the heavy smoke to the ground. Rushing toward the makeshift fort, George dropped his rifle and picked up the National flag,from another man down. The thought of using a bayonet disturbed him immensely. Scrambling over thick brush, barricades, and walls, George made his way to the center of the turmoil to find the flagstaff, and he began to hoist the colors. The firing was still intense. A scraggly, ill-clad man in a shabby gray jacket charged at him. George reached around to the small of his back and felt the pistol. After he pulled it out from behind, he raised it in front of him toward the charging Reb. The Rebs eyes glowed with anger, looking straight into George, ready to take his soul. He pulled back the hammer and let go. The sound was much louder than the rifle because of the short barrel. A puff of smoke whiffed into George's face. The Reb was still coming, his eyes large and fierce with pain and determination. George cocked again and let loose. Another loud crack, and the man went down. George stood there, looked at the dead man and then at his pistol. He had seen death, but he had never until this moment thought of himself as the cause. The rifle kept things at a distance.

Finally, a hand descended on his shoulder from behind. He swirled around with tears hot and burning. He was about to shoot again when someone said, "It's over! Them Rebs hightailed it." It was William, pulling at his hand to help raise the flag. "We're the first in."

"And now we're gonna go get 'em," Blunt inserted. "There's three more forts we gotta capture."

George just stood there, his only feeling a heavy, sodden dullness. Slowly and methodically, he started to return the pistol to the small of his back. Then unexpectedly, he dropped it and wiped the corners of his eyes with the back of his hands. Others were starting to converge on George and the hoisted National flag. Lieutenant Colonel Potter was one of them, a short man with a square wall of a forehead and heavy brows for a base. He banged George on the back and said, "Good job, son." They had split the Fifty-first, Colonel Ferero taking half to outflank the enemy and Colonel Potter rushing the fort. Colonel Potter looked down at the gun, bent over, snatched it, flipped it over his back, and caught it. "Nice pistol," he exclaimed. Then Sergeant Blunt said, "Another confiscated weapon. Put it with the others we've taken in this action."

Blunt took the pistol, his eyes squinting with amusement toward George. "Sometimes ya gotta leave things on the battlefield and move on, Mr. Everson," said Blunt.

Chapter 7

Weir's Point

Jacob was gone. A man lay in front of him dead, shot by the pistol he had won in a poker game. More of his comrades lay in the field behind him. Yet the assault had been successful. They would again split the troops for an attack on the fort in the middle of the island. The wounded were already coming in to a small house captured just minutes before. Some came on stretchers, and some were walking. The men stood around like posts, rifles across their shoulders, free arms hanging rigid, all waiting. General Reno would take half the brigade with part of the Fifty-first New York around the right wing again, and Colonel Potter would take the other half with F Company around the left side. They went back into the woods and knee-deep in swamp mud again. Sergeant Blunt stood by one of the barricades with his hands on his hips. He bent his torso backward until his spine cracked and waited for the young lieutenant to approach. His face red from the cold, Blunt held his hands behind his immense back as he started talking very low. George was between them barely able to hear what was going on.

"Sir," Blunt spewed quietly, trying to keep the men from listening. He continued spitting the "s" between his teeth, "Ya can't do that. Ya'll get nuthin' out of it 'cept killin' all the men."

"I know what I'm doing," the lieutenant said as he held up a quieting hand. "Now get the men ready." For a moment, the two stood looking at each other, anger hanging in the air between them like an invisible sword. Then Blunt gave a whirling salute and stamped his feet in a left turn. With a thud, Blunt slapped his fist into his other hand as he approached George, William, and the others.

"We're ta double-quick time ta the next fort and then rush it," Blunt told his men. "Seems a Capin' Wright from A Company got the credit for a takin' this here fort first." Then looking at George, he gave him a "keep your mouth shut" look. Blunt turned and stared with deadly concentration toward the departing lieutenant. The haggard company of men started their march toward the fort in the middle of the island. The going was rough through the dense woods. A few of the men swore as tree limbs snapped back, let loose by unthinking comrades. The rain had let up, but they continued to march, still wet with canteens bumping and rifles pushed in front of their faces to avoid slamming branches. Conversation was minimal this time, but William turned to George and said, "I heard something like this happened to Blunt during the Mexican War. Someone down there got all his men shot up wanting to make a name for himself." George had heard the same from Jacob. Jacob, his friend, his teacher, his mentor. Now Jacob was gone. Pain and loneliness walked with him through the trees and the mud. George knew Blunt, but he didn't know the lieutenant. Something inside told him what Blunt was planning to do. Kill the lieutenant during the charge.

After an hour they arrived at a clearing. The forced march was supposed to drive the Rebs toward the fort, clearing all in their path like a giant broom. They had arrived before the others. Now without any rest or plan, they had to attack the fort or battery of large guns— Weir's Point. Again the men heard the *cracks* and *pops* and the buzzing overhead. They flattened themselves out to the ground. Then came the call to charge. Men grumbled to their feet and did as they were ordered. Out of the corner of his eye, George saw Blunt, pistol in hand, taking aim. Men were still rushing in lunatic flight toward destruction. George was on one knee, aiming with his newfound rifle. Knowing what he had to do to stop Blunt, he got up reluctantly, hating himself. He'd save the sergeant from his own destruction, or he'd let him do what he would and then watch a firing squad blast away the life out of Blunt. George rushed toward Blunt, rifle still aimed at the fort, and with blinding speed, he smacked him in the side with all his weight, knocking both of them to the ground. "Whad th' blazes yuh doin', boy?" Blunt exclaimed, panting to get his breath. George gazed toward the fort, which was slowly disappearing in a cloud of gunpowder smoke. He could not see the lieutenant. A strange, cold fear filled George's being. *Oh, God!* he thought, *I'm too late. He's killed the lieutenant.*

"Ged up, boy!" Blunt said. "We're supposed to be chargin' that there fort."

"But First Sergeant," exclaimed George, "the lieutenant?"

"Wadja think? I was a shootin' at him?"

"You had words."

"Ain't no need ta worry none. Them fools git their own selves kilt. They're glory hounds. 'Sides, wad difference duz it make to yuh?"

Pushing his bottom lip forward in thought, George remarked, "I don't know."

Blunt eyed George and then said, "Yur a sodjer."

George stared with a combination of defiance and stupidity. Blunt winked and said, "Git. We might make a soldier outa yuh yet."

That knowing look, that smirking wink was worse than— Then George bolted to rush the fort with the others. Another *buzzz* overhead.

Finally, the firing had stopped, and the smoke started to drift away. The Fifty-first was again the first in with the colors. Again, the wounded sent on their way—this time to Ashby's Point back toward the boats. The others massed together for a charge to the head of the island, where the remaining force of Rebs had concentrated in two camps. They needed a small detachment to do another sweep around the right of the island. Blunt found his volunteers, including George and William.

Tromping through mud and trees again, they soon found a captured column of about sixty Rebs who had been trying to make their escape through Shallow Bag Bay. Escorting them back, and in the front was the young lieutenant.

"Yuh see," Blunt said and turned toward George. "He gits his glory, and now he'll git his pat on the back like a good sodjer from General Reno or Colonel Ferero."

"You're not bitter?" asked George.

"Naw. He'll git his," Blunt said. "But my job is to see that my men ain't anywhere around when he does."

When they met up with the rest of the regiment, they found that the fortress and camp had surrendered to General Reno, bringing the count of prisoners to more than two thousand. The fighting had lasted more than four hours. Some of the men had already started campfires and were brewing coffee and cooking their hard tack in the little pork they had. George looked down at his hard tack and saw something move.

"This is the hardest stuff I've ever handled, and now there's vermin in it," he said to William.

Another older soldier looked at him in disbelief. "Thems jest bow-weevels. Think of it as fresh meat." Bugs had infested the two-by-two-inch hard cracker. "Normally," the old soldier continued, "we just fry everything in this here pork fat. Makes a mighty tasty meal … if you can get it down."

"Isn't that part of your canteen you're frying with?" George questioned.

"Yup. These here things are so badly welded together they leak. We jest split one in half and make it into a frying pan. Water's where you find it."

Unsure why exactly, George started to walk toward Sergeant Blunt, who was propped up against a tree, stirring a smaller fire and staring toward the north. George remained uncomfortably still as if waiting for Blunt to speak. The older man scooped out tobacco from a small pouch. George wondered how he had kept it dry through all this. He lit his pipe with a burning stick from the small fire and eyed George through the flame. Blowing smoke, he followed the trail with his eyes. Then pointing his pipe like a pistol toward the head of the island, he said, "We're gonna take Elizabeth City tomorrow." He continued to point with his pipe toward the south. "And then we're gonna get back on the boats and take some other places south of us. North Carolina."

"Back on the boats," George said and sighed.

"Yup. We got them Rebs so baffled they don't know which way we're cumin' or where we'll be next."

The next day George was assigned to regimental headquarters as a runner. His duties were to deliver messages as fast as his legs would take him from the company commanders to the regimental commander, General Reno. However, it wasn't just his legs. General Reno wanted to deliver a message to Colonel Hawkins of the Ninth Regiment in another brigade. This meant getting on another boat with the half of the regiment that was pulling out to attack Elizabeth City to the north. He embarked among several steamships surrounded by small gunboats. Eventually, he found that the colonel was on the boat just opposite his. So he waited. Up until now, the runner business had been good for him because the runners ate the same rations as the officers, but not at the same time. After an hour or so, the men spotted land. It would not be long before they reached their target, Elizabeth City. Hugging the coastline and pulling closer, they sighted the port. Something unusual was happening that made George stare over the side of the boat. On the wharf there was a black woman flaying her arms about and motioning for them to land. The whole fleet of small vessels was at a standstill, using every bit of caution. Without warning, a volley came toward the boats, splinters everywhere. Men recklessly scrambled for the other side, ducking and crawling. Then the howitzers from the small gunboats opened up on buildings adjacent to the wharf where the firing was coming from. The firing from the warehouses dwindled, and the men started pouring to the shoreside of the boat, firing their rifles toward the little storehouses. "Look at them spinters fly," yelled one riflemen. George saw the gaping holes they were making. The buildings were fast becoming shambles. "Cease fire!" came the command, and as abruptly as it had started, it was all over. Men were jumping onto the wharf where the woman miraculously still stood, and some were crouching and moving toward the small warehouses. "Them Rebs took off, sir," came back a report. Immediately, a whole company of men was ready to charge the small city. Racing for the town, they found haversacks, canteens, rifles, and even cookware dropped in the hasty retreat. George had debarked with the rest of the troops and found himself near Colonel Hawkins, the regimental commander to whom he was to deliver his message. Beside him were two captains, one on each arm of the very large woman who had beckoned them on the wharf. Shaking and crying, she told them, "My masta warned me. They said that they wan't gonna let nobody live at all, but was goin' to kill every one of us."

"Gentlemen," Colonel Hawkins said, addressing the captains and other officers surrounding him, "I infer from this that we were to receive no quarter. So be it. Take your companies and set fire to any storehouses and quarters the rebels were using."

The officers looked bewildered. During the war so far, no one had done such a thing. George knew that the colonel didn't need to explain himself, and an order was an order. Colonel Hawkins looked at his men and continued, "Enemy forces have been raised and supported by the buildings you are about to destroy, and they have been used by the States in rebellion for the purpose of subverting the Constitution and the laws of the United States. Now let the woman go and get busy."

The officers hurriedly turned and went about doing exactly that, burning the buildings. One was heard muttering to the other officer, "I think the old man is just mad 'cause they tried to make him a fool."

The next command shocked George even more. They were to get back on the boats and head back to Roanoke. The colonel felt no need to stay since there was nothing left standing. That had been Elizabeth City. A relief came over George. He did not want to be stuck here any longer than he was. Finally, Colonel Hawkins turned to George, "Who are you again?" George promptly handed him the envelope and waited for a reply. "Well," Colonel Hawkins said, "we'll both tell General Reno when we get back what I'm going to do about this message." That seemed reasonable to George since they were all heading back anyway. Later George would find out the message informed the colonel about a meeting with General Burnside and all the commanders the next evening. Returning to his friends and the campfire sounded good to George right about now. Being a runner for the regiment had its advantages, but not today.

BATTLE OF
NEW BERNE, N.C.

North: 90 Killed; 384 wounded, 1 missing
South: 71 Killed; 106 wounded, 413 captured
51st NY: 71 killed or wounded

Chapter 8

New Berne

Scores of men were sick and getting sicker. The men were given some fruit in small quantities to ward off scurvy. Mostly there was hard tack, which had to be soaked in order to bite into it.

"I got to go on sick call again," a new recruit told George. "That's the third time in three weeks. They'll have you down on the black list as a malingerer," George responded. The dreadful little black list the first sergeant kept was for extra duty for those he thought needed it. Anyone who didn't get along was put on the black list. George had been on it many times.

"It's those dang Tennessee trots. I been headin' to the woods all day. Ain't no outhouses here, or I'd be there all day. They been gettin' to me. Must be something I 'et," the recruit said.

"More soldiers are in the sick call line because of sick stomachs than anything else lately. The doctors are passing out bellybands to tie around the stomach. They hope that'll take the problem away," said George.

"Yup, or else they just say we're homesick and send us back to quarters. So I reckon you're right. I'll just live with it. 'Cause I'm even smart 'nuff to know their ole stuff don't work." One week passed, and the orderly sergeant arranged a medical discharge for the recruit, "Too sick for duty." George found out later the recruit had died on the way home.

After thirty days on Roanoke Island, living on salt pork, hard tack, and coffee, more men were being discharged or dying from camp fever than those who were killed in the battle. The feeling around the camps was that if something didn't happen soon, they would be building rafts and using poles to get home. The time finally came when they would move back to the boats, make a landing south, and take New Berne, North Carolina.

"It won't be as easy this time," William commented. "They've had a chance to get recruits in."

"We've spent more time sitting around than fighting," said George. "Forget the boats. I'll swim, wade, or walk. I'm ready to get out of here."

"Ya need ta," said William. "You're beginning to look a little peaked. Been ta see the doc?"

"Nah. All's they do is give you salts ... and then laudanum. Stuff'll lay ya up for days."

The weather was still chilly, and rain was in the air. The restless men started packing up their gear and moving toward the boats to embark. However, it would not be the same arduous task of going through Hatteras Inlet. The sea was in their favor this time because the tides had helped make the passage a good eight feet deep. They crept in single file, moving like slugs. The Fifty-first was loaded on the steamers *Lancer* and the *Pioneer*. All vessels rendezvoused at Hatteras Inlet, made their preparations, and then moved on. The next night, anchoring off the mouth of Slocum's Creek in the Neuse River just fourteen miles from New Berne, the packed vessels waited for the rain to stop. William turned to George and said, "In the morning I ain't waitin' for no boat. At least we can sleep on land, rain or not."

In the morning the sun tried to break through. The steamers started to ground themselves, but many of the men were like William, too impatient for boats. They started wading ashore, holding their cartridge boxes above their heads. The Fifty-first New York was the first to plant their colors on shore. The men quickly rallied around their flags. By nightfall twelve thousand had landed. Six cannons were unloaded, but the roads were muddy and torn up by the howitzers that had been firing from ships since early morning. The all-night task of moving inland was detailed to the Fifty-first Pennsylvania, the Twenty-first Massachusetts, Fifty-first New York, and Ninth New Jersey. About three thousand men started their long, arduous march in that order. After four miles and one and a half hours, they reached some railroad tracks. This was where they were to bivouac for the night and prepare to march north along the tracks toward New Berne at early light. This brigade, which was made of four regiments, would push the enemy's flank toward the other regiments that would also be pushing northward. Then they would encircle and capture what they believed to be about two thousand Rebs.

People started small campfires in a long line of deserted trenches abandoned by the enemy, and again the men devoured the staples issued to each man of hard tack, beans, coffee, and fried pork fat. The surgeon making his rounds insisted the men broil their small issue of meat instead of frying it in great gobs of grease. He called it "death by the frying pan." After he would leave, comments arose, such as, "What's that butcher know anyway?" and back they would go to cooking their way. George and William watched with amazement as the men around him shoveled in their whole issue of food. "It's this way before any battle," one older man answered his silent question, and the subject was dropped. Some had their own recipe of soaking the hard tack in water and then frying it in deep fat and calling it hell-fire stew.

An officer unfamiliar to George made his way through the encamped men, one who had a strong, dauntless air about him. As he approached the men around George, they all started to rise. "No," he said, "please stay seated."

"Good evening, sir," some of the men offered.

"I'm Chaplain Benton," he introduced himself. "I thought I'd come by and chat. See how things are going."

One side of George was feeling uncomfortable. It was so easy for a minister to utter platitudes and false comforts. In spite of his notion, like it or not, his mind returned to Cayuga County—to Sarah, Jane, John, and his father and mother. This chaplain brought a calm feeling. He had a force about him, a great presence born of certainty, much like George's father, who had been a lay preacher back in Moravia. George's spirit soared. Just listening to this man, he knew again he was doing the right thing. After Jacob's death, questions had flooded his inner thoughts about killing another human. He wanted to confess to the chaplain that a man had been lost at sea because of his selfishness of keeping a pistol. Now he decided he could atone for that mistake by fighting the enemy the best he could. The talking became easier even for William, the New York City street hustler, whom George thought had only one religion, gambling. In spite of the chaplain and his encouragement and prayers, it still rained all night. Sleep was not easy. One of the younger men with a harmonica started playing, and before long, several others were singing or whistling. It was a familiar ballad, but George had not paid much attention to the words before. "Just before the Battle, Mother" never had so much significance until now.

Just before the battle, mother,

I am thinking most of you,

While upon the field we're watching

With the enemy in view.

Comrades brave are 'round me lying,

Filled with thoughts of home and God

For well they know that on the morrow,

Some will sleep beneath the sod.

CHORUS

Farewell, mother, you may never

Press me to your heart again,

But oh, you'll not forget me, mother,

If I'm numbered with the slain.

Oh, I long to see you, mother

And the loving ones at home,

But I'll never leave our banner

Till in honor I can come.

Tell the traitors all around you

That their cruel words we know,

In every battle kill our soldiers

By the help they give the foe.

Hear the battle cry of freedom,

How it swells upon the air.

Oh, yes, we'll rally 'round the standard,

Or we'll perish nobly there.

Roanoke had gone fast as expected. Rumor had it that this time there was more reinforcements on the other side, which might make it a little tougher. The rain started to let up, and as George heard the last line, "Farewell, mother, you may never press me to your heart again," he could taste salt from the wetness of his face. As the chaplain left, George could barely make out in the darkness that this marble statue of a man was dabbing his eyes with the corners of his sleeve.

In the middle of the night, the boat howitzers started shelling, trying to "soften up" the enemy, as they called it, before the charge in the morning. Before dawn men from Company D were thrown out in front as skirmishers, trying to find weak spots. With the dawn came a fog as thick as the gunpowder clouds at the last battle. At his vantage point toward the front, George could barely make out through his sleep-craved eyes the figure of Colonel Ferrero, the regimental commander, and a lieutenant colonel about to disappear into the fog toward the woods directly in front of them. Suddenly, a *crack* rang out, and one of the figures fell to the ground. George could now see that Colonel Ferrero was dragging the other man back. Instantly, dozens of others joined them, trying to get them to the safety of the ravines. The injured man was Lieutenant Colonel Potter, but he was up and calling for his men to rally without looking at his wound or the seriousness of it. It seemed like yesterday—not a month ago—that the same buzzing sounds had been flying overhead. After he talked to an officer, Sergeant Blunt ran to where George and the others were ducking and trying to dodge the flying balls, knowing what damage they could do to a body.

"Awright," Blunt shouted over the incoming projectiles. "Here's wat's goin' on. We was s'posed to be to the right of the enemy. We ain't! The colonels made a reconnaissance. They say we got rifle pits that extend a mile upwards of the railroad tracks. They got deep ravines and fallen timber in front and a swamp. There may be a dozen or more of them there redans full of riflemen, and they says we got maybe five big guns aimed right at us."

"A redan? Sergeant?" came a question.

"A trench, ya moron," said Blunt. "There be plenty of 'em between us and the railroad tracks. Now boys, yore gonna find out what a sodjer's made of."

The evil cloud of fog with projectiles flying from it played havoc on the thousand men lined and ready just minutes ago. Some were cringing in the grass. Others were running in complete disorder. An explosion would come from the fog. Then a thud would come, and another man would fall. The Fifty-first New York was ordered to move forward along the railroad tracks with the Twenty-first Massachusetts on their right, the Ninth New Jersey on their left, and the Fifty-first Pennsylvania following. Slowly, the thousand men inched forward, blindly firing into the sinister fog.

Chapter 9

The Railroad Tracks

William was beside George, loading, firing, and inching forward. One would bob his head above a small ridge and fire, and then the other would repeat the pattern. This battle was much worse than Roanoke. It was madness. Men were running into one another, trying to escape the unending volley from the Rebs.

"William," George shouted, "you ever seen a turkey shoot? They pop up, and you shoot at 'em."

"No, but I think from what I've been told, we're the turkeys."

"William, you got a nasty way of turning things around at the wrong time."

"I know odds," said William, "and ours ain't so good."

Another man beside George was hit and went down. Even with the cover of the ridges or redans, the Rebs were randomly hitting marks. Both sides were firing blindly, first through the fog and now through the heavy black powder that hung in the air. The mud caused by the all-night rain made moving even slower. Cannon fire increased. Explosions went off all around them. Blunt had said there were more than a dozen canons pointed their way. There had been rumors that five thousand more new troops were waiting on the other side. George looked back at the wounded lying on the ground. He had stepped over at least four and kept firing. Orderlies were tearing open the blouses and shirts of some of the fallen, getting up, and moving among the others.

"What are they doing?" George questioned aloud. Then he got his gruesome answer from Blunt, who had slipped up behind him. "They's tearing, lookin' for belly wounds. If they got one, they leave 'em. Yuh ain't got a prayer with a belly wound. Might jest as well leave the fellow a pistol. Let him blow his own brains out."

George blinked in astonished silence and then turned and loaded again, this time with the unsettling thought of being hit. Then it finally dawned on him that he had been very lucky so far. Then he tripped. The hulk of a man beneath him was the chaplain. Here was a person that George thought could not be hurt. Last night this man had so much control and a competent way of handling himself. Yet here he lay, gone, with such terrible suddenness. Blunt pulled George up by the back of his collar. George felt himself frozen. Blunt pushed. George took a quick intake of breath like someone about to plunge into icy water. Dead and wounded men were lying in all directions. He reached for another round in his cartridge pouch. He felt seven. He'd started with forty and had picked up another pouch. Racing toward a ridge for cover, he had the startling realization that they were all running low on ammunition. The sheer madness of it all was driving men into the ground. A part of him wanted to dive into the grass and mud with them. Pull the earth up over his head as a small child does a blanket, waiting for the boogieman to go away. The buzzing overhead, the explosions, dirt flying everywhere, fragments of debris and metal tearing everything in their path continued. George's ears were ringing, and he was fighting to walk, sometimes knee-deep in mud. Methodically, as if in some trance, his rifle would come to his shoulder, and he would fire. Each time he loaded, it took him about a minute, maybe two. He had no sure way to estimate time, but having shot off thirty-three rounds and another cartridge box so far, it was maybe about one and a half hours. *How much more of this can there be?* he thought. He felt for another round. Only three! Another dead man. It was a lieutenant from another company. The top of his head was gone as if a surgeon had neatly removed it. His sword was still in his hand, but his arm lay about a foot from his body.

George felt the strong sensation in his own stomach. Something lurched. A convulsion jerked upwards and out. George threw up. He felt his knees struggling to pull his body forward.

"Yuh okay?" Blunt was hollering at him. Pushing George toward the ground, Blunt hurriedly explained that the Fifty-first Pennsylvania, which had been waiting behind in reserve, would fire one volley, and then they would all charge. Penned to the ground now, George watched as a storm of men came up to where they were, all firing and shouting. With bayonets extended, they charged over and toward the strongholds of the enemy.

"See that?" Blunt shouted again. "They's running! Gid up, boy. Les go."

Strength pumped through George's body, making him leap up and run forward with the rest. He was astounded by his own enthusiasm. It was relief enough to know that someone else had come to the rescue just at the moment when the depths of despair were about to engulf him. Running forward, he heard the *crack* and then felt the burning in his leg. This time there was no buzzing sound, just the bite from the bee. Then the sensation of heat started to spread, down the leg and up the leg. George did not stop, could not stop.

There was a great deal of chaos as the rebel side was fleeing across the railroad bridge and the road bridge, leaving blankets, knapsacks, arms, and anything else that might be heavy. After their retreat, the rebels had set afire the railroad bridge and destroyed part of the other. They could chase no farther for now.

The fog was lifting along with the heavy smoke. George had miscalculated. They had been fighting for four hours and had pushed back a mile and a half of riflemen. As George stood there, resting, he watched a large bellow of smoke rise in the sky to his right. In their retreat the rebels must have set fire to the whole town. Gripping his leg, he felt the sticky cloth of his trousers.

"George!" It was William. "You've been hit."

George looked at his gooey red hand. His trousers were torn, and there was the semblance of a gash on his thigh. An orderly assigned to the ambulance company gave him a cloth to put over it and told him it wasn't that bad. "Just a scratch. Nowhere near as bad as this here fellow," he said, pointing to a dead boy dressed in gray.

"Looks like someone took a hammer and pounded his chest in," blurted William. Then he turned and threw up.

The battle was over. Now came the cleanup. The Fifty-first New York's assignment was to rebuild the railroad bridge and then guard it, opening up supply routes. More than a hundred men killed in four hours and another four hundred wounded. General Burnside had sent two hundred or more prisoners north for detainment and released the prisoners belonging to the city on their parole. Fugitives from the surrounding towns and plantations were overrunning the town. William had told George after the battle the town was as quiet as a New England village. For the black people, the town of New Berne meant freedom. Two of the refuge slaves reported they had escaped and were living in the swamps.

Not all shared the enterprise of reliving the battle around the campfires. There was the future. Burnside's Army was now making plans to take Fort Macon, which was farther south. George's small wound was getting better, but his stomach ailment seemed to grow more severe each passing day. Blunt finally made a compassionate decision. He gave George a furlough for the wound he'd received.

Chapter 10

Furlough

George received a railroad pass, and he started his long journey home, torn with emotion. He had left the friends he had shared life and death with, but he was going home to his family. His father, mother, Sarah, Jane, and John absorbed his every thought. He felt guilty—guilty because Jacob and hundreds of others would never see the trees changing colors, their home, their families, the lilacs, or another sunrise. Exhaustion overcame him, and he slept the whole first day of the train ride toward home. In two weeks he would turn seventeen. How ironic it would be if his father would not give him permission to go back. He was still underage. He had fought in two major battles, lost friends, and had killed a fellow human being, and yet he still needed parental consent. For now, he would be content that he was going to trade his hard tack, beans, and coffee for a good home-cooked meal. Thoughts of roasted turkey, cranberries, potatoes, corn on the cob, giblet gravy, hot rolls, and mincemeat pie made his mouth water.

"Hey, mister," a young voice awakened him. "You been in the war?" The boy was loaded with oranges, peanuts, magazines, and newspapers. Many called the peddler the "train butch." His muffed blond hair seemed to stick straight up in the back, and bangs fell down to his wide eyes, waiting for George to answer.

"Yeah," George replied and then yawned. "Been in about a year now."

"Looks like yuh was wounded," the boy edged on. "Didja kill anybody? See anybody git kilt? I'm gonna join up pretty soon."

George felt he had enough of this one-sided conversation and decided to shorten it by buying one of the day-old newspapers from him. The boy strutted through the carriage, eagerly dropping magazines, dime novels, and some maps beside weary travelers. He would be back, vending his overpriced goods after dinner. George casually looked down at his paper and found on the front page an article and picture of none other than General Ambrose Burnside flamboyantly garnishing his long whiskers down the side of his face. The article read something like the dime novel the older man sitting across from him was reading. Noticing the man, George couldn't help but observe that he, too, was growing hair like General Burnside. Probably just a fast passing thing, but he thought the general might start a new fashion among men. *Maybe*, he thought, *they'll call them burnsides after the general ... or sideburns.* However, he believed it would never catch on, feeling his own silky smooth face. He had made shaving his peach fuzz a habit to conceal his age, but even now he really didn't have to.

Three days into the journey, George felt as he had when he marched through snow from Washington to Annapolis. The seats were hard, and the conductor was constantly crying, "Tickets, tickets," after every depot. If the conductor wasn't calling for tickets, he was throwing off deadheads who were looking for a free ride. The excitement in him was aroused when he reckoned that the amazing speed of this iron horse would mean that he would be back to where he had started a year ago in only four days. Then just a short walk or maybe a buggy ride from the depot would take him to the outskirts of town and home.

The train rolled to a stop. Steam gushed out the sides, and finally, George saw the familiar old station. Walking the rest of the way on the old dirt road, he approached his house. John had freshly whitewashed the small picket fence. His mother stood in the doorway, wiping her hands on her apron, fidgeting. When she saw him, the tears rolled down her cheeks. The first words from his mother's mouth after all the hugs were, "George, you look so poorly. Have you eaten anything?" And so the fattening process began. His father, forsaking his statue-like pose, finally smiled, blessed that he had his boy back in one piece. Soon after, the rest of the family converged on George like a whirlwind—Sarah, Jane, and John.

The small talk soon shifted to the large dining table, where George feasted, savoring the fresh biscuits that rolled in his mouth, so unlike the hard tack he'd had to soak. Succulent, mouthwatering white turkey slid down his throat, and butter oozed through his fingers as he devoured corn on the cob.

After dinner he positioned himself as far back in the porch rocker as he could to ease the bloated feeling of overindulgence and gazed out at the flickering stars. No war here, just peace, home, and family. Sarah, Jane, and John soon situated themselves around George to hear of his escapades. George was silent.

"George," Sarah broke the silence, "are you going back?"

"I don't know, Sarah," he said. He pondered the question some more, knowing that he would be only seventeen this month. His father had just finished a conversation on the same theme. "I can get you out, George, because you're underage," Mr. Everson had told him, eyes staring at the floor. Things had not been going so well at home. His father was thinking about moving as soon as the war died down, probably to Ohio where there was more land. "But," his father continued, "I guess you're a man now, being a soldier and all. If you need me to get you out, I will." He left it at that.

George saw how John was getting enthusiastic over the adventure. He quickly tried to explain the hardships, but he remembered that a lifetime ago he, too, was excited. John was only thirteen and much smaller than George, with no chance of pulling off the trick he had used. This war had to end soon. Would he go back? There were too many lives already lost. He stared past the stars into his own thoughts.

Epilogue

The personal letters are from actual accounts of a great-great-uncle during his service of the Civil War with the Fifty-first New York Volunteers. Burnside was best known for his failure as the general of the Potomac, not of his success to help bring the Confederate supply line to a standstill. A lot of the actual trench warfare and training are from my own experiences during the Vietnam era. War does not change, just the weapons. Other letters from official records came from General Ambrose E. Burnside (US. Army); Brigadier General Jesse Reno (US Army), who commanded the Second Brigade; and Colonel Edward Ferrero, who commanded Fifty-first New York Volunteers. The expedition was led by General Burnside prior to his command of the Potomac. The Army took Roanoke Island, Elizabeth City, and Newbern to cut the Confederate supply route and to enforce the embargo against the South. Although George Everson was real, most of his exploits are purely fictitious.

During the war, unsanitary living conditions and poor rations were common. Ignorance was abundant, and bathing was not that common. Thousands would drink from the same stream in which they bathed. Most men slept, worked, and fought in the same clothes, never changing, not even for bed. They seldom washed eating utensils, and even when the utensils were covered with week-old food, the soldiers used them repeatedly. During the first part of the war, the Federal Army of the Potomac reported that 640 out of every thousand men contracted dysentery. The next year the rate was 995 per thousand. The death rate from dysentery remained low compared with the toll from typhoid fever. Perhaps one-fourth of the noncombatant deaths was the result of this disease, commonly called "camp fever."

Glossary

Blouse	Jacket soldiers wore as part of uniform.
Bowling	People played this game on bowling greens as early as 1800, but they later became known as bowling alleys. The game of ninepin was banned because it was associated with gambling. Ten-pin bowling was started around 1839. Supposedly, one more pin stopped the gambling.
Bull	Lying. Started as slang with soldiers during Civil War.
Calaboose	Jail.
Camp fever	Typhoid.
Howitzer	Cannon.
Laudanum	Opium, usually sold over the counter in liquid form, used to help control mild pain. Abuse spread quickly, and many people were hooked.
National	Word used for "Union."
News butch	Young boy on the railroads who sold newspapers, magazines, and snacks.
Orderly	A soldier assigned in administrative capacity. An orderly sergeant did not have as much authority as a regular sergeant.

Redan   Trench, ravine, gully, gorge, or ditch.

Sutler   Merchant appointed by government, one per regiment, to supply troops in the field with pastries, tobacco, and other things. Goods were sold on credit, and the cost was deducted from the soldiers' pay. Sutlers' prices were usually very high, and they followed the troops wherever they went.

Three-cent piece Popular coin from 1851 to 1873, very small.

Minie' Ball   It was named after the French Army Officer Claude Minie' and quickly nicknamed the mini ball. It was cylindrical in a shape we know as the bullet but much larger and fatter than anything used today. It was one inch long and a half inch in diameter, almost hollow, and it was made from soft lead, which made it expand on impact. Traveling at less than the speed of sound gave it a whistling, humming sound rather than the familiar *pop* we hear today from bullets breaking the sound barrier. At this slow speed, it caused even more damage with a *ripple* effect when it hit a person (which was like getting hit twice).

Bugle Calls

Reveille	Time to get up.
Tattoo	Lights out, get ready for bed.
Taps	Your head should be in the pillow.

There is a bugle call for everything, and a different tune for each purpose—mail, charge, retreat, flag raising, flag lowering, assembly, and of course, mealtime.

How the Units Were Formed during Civil War

Company	Comprised of a hundred men, captain commanding.
Regiment	Ten companies, 1,046 men, colonel commanding
Brigade	Four regiments, brigadier general (one star)
Division	Three brigades, lieutenant general (two stars)

Hard Tack   Well used on the Union side, this was hard bread in the shape of a cracker, three inches by three inches and a half of an inch thick. They were so hard that soldiers had to soak or fry them before they were able to bite into them. They were usually infested with weevils or other types of worms.

Bibliography and Suggested Readings

Billings, John Davis. *Hard Tack and Coffee,* George M. Smith and Co, Boston, 1889

Cox, Clinton. *Undying Glory, The Story of the Massachusetts 54th Regiment.* New York: Scholastic, Inc., 1991

Donald, David Herbert, ed. *Gone for a Soldier: The Civil War Memoirs of Private Alfred Billard.* Boston: Alec Thomas Archives, 1975.

Fleischman, Paul. *Bull Run.* New York: HarperCollins, 1993.

Hamilton, Virginia. *The House of Dies Drear.* Canada: Collier, 1968.

Keith, Harold. *Rifles for Watie.* New York: HarperCollins, 1957.

McCutcheon, Marc. *Everyday Life in the 1800's.* Cincinnati, OH: Writer's Digest Books, 1993.

Murphy, Jim. *The Boy's War: Confederate and Union Soldiers Talk about the Civil War.* New York: Scholastic, Inc., 1990.

Ray, Delia. *Behind the Blue and Gray: The Soldier's Life in the Civil War.* New York: Scholastic, Inc., 1991.

Scott, Robert N., LTC, comp., *The War of the Rebellion:, A Compilation of the Official Records of the Union and Confederate Armies.; Lieut. Col. Robert N. Scott, Published Pursuant to Act of Congress Approved June 6, 1880.*N.p.: n.p., n.d. Print.

Steele, William O. *The Perilous Road.* Orlando, FL: Harcourt Brace Jananovich, 1958.

Thomas, Emory M., PhD. "The Lost Confederates of Roanoke." *Civil War Magazine* April 1993.

Tenting Tonight. The Soldier's Life (Time-Life American Civil War Series). Alexandria, VA: Time-Life Books, 1984.

Edwards Brothers Malloy
Thorofare, NJ USA
September 22, 2016